Castle Rock

and

Other Poems

Of

Mountains

By

Bruce C. Autry
Margaret Autry
Michael Autry

Dedication

For Sharon, Melissa, Mary, Michael, and Margaret—my beloved wife and our four children who put up with me through the good times and sad times.

ISBN: 9798842790609
Imprint: Independently published.

Preface

This collection contains poems going back as far as 1996 and coming down to 2022. Many of the poems are autobiographical, but many are dramatic lyrics with the speakers having only a casual connection to myself. I refer mainly to some of the romantic lyrics which play upon the Phantom of the Opera. This persona seemed appropriate for the turmoil associated with passion and unrequited love.

Although I have written long poems, short stories, and novels, I believe that my real talent lies with lyric poetry. It was my childhood dream to be a poet, and I think I have fulfilled that dream. I have received many compliments for my verse which most readers have found accessible. Like Robert Frost, I am a poet who wants to be understood, and I have fulfilled that goal.

The poets I admire most are Robert Frost, Emily Dickinson, William Carlos Williams, William Shakespeare, John Keats, William Blake, William Wordsworth, Samuel Taylor Coleridge,

Robert Browning, Alfred, Lord Tennyson, and Walt Whitman.

I spent many years working on a dissertation exploring the origins of Romantic poetry in the Evangelical Revival of the 18th century. I read so many primary sources such as the sermons of John Wesley and George Whitefield; the devotional works of William Law, James Hervey, and so many more that I can't remember. I devoted chapters to the poetry of William Cowper, William Blake, William Wordsworth, and Samuel Taylor Coleridge.

The stresses and strains of full-time teaching and trying to finish the dissertation led me into a severe depression which has never fully disappeared, but I look back at my long life and feel more joy than sorrow. All in all, I have accomplished more than most writers, so I leave my works to those who have enjoyed them. That is enough for me.

Table of Contents

I. Poems by Bruce C. Autry

1. My Celtic Girl   9
2. Real Estate   10
3. Mexican Smoke   11
4. Remember the Alamo   12
5. The Last Lament   13
6. Somewhere in Time   14
7. The Wind of Skye   15
8. A Gentle Rain   16
9. Ungifted Gift   17
10. My Green Beret   18
11. My Three Brothers   19
12. The Woman That I Loved   20
13. Too Late   21
14. Flora's Dream   23
15. Flora's Fling   24
16. The Tower   25
17. Flora's Grave   26
18. A Winged Fortune Cookie   27
19. The Comfort of Quilts   30
20. When You Leave   31
21. The Phantom's Death   32
22. The Rose of All Time   33
23. Change   34
24. Foretaste of Hell   35
25. Liar's Club   36
26. Lost in Time   37
27. The Gift   38
28. Books and Other Oddities of Love   40
29. The Walker   42
30. My Paternal Grandmother   44
31. My Maternal Grandmother   46

32. My Paternal Grandfather   48
33. My Maternal Grandfather 50
34. Dead Bird   52
35. Femme Fatale   53
36. Twilight Love   55
37. In Memoriam: Karla Faye Tucker   57
38. The Waterfall   59
39. Heavenly Justice   60
40. Ripe Cherries   62
41. Masks   63
42. Seasonal Magic   64
43. Choices: For the Season of Lent   65
44. Let It Go   66
45. Pieces   67
46. Mule Deer   68
47. Castle Rock   69
48. The Gothic Bookshop   70
49. Parkinson's   72
50. Viva la Vida   73
51. The Old Home Place   74
52. Risqué   76

II. A. Poems by Margaret Autry

53. Good Morning   78
54. FML-8/20/20   79
55. Untitled-12/24/20   80
56. Hope-6/26/21   81
57. Lucky-7/2/21   82
58. Can I Take a Trip to Heaven-11/11/21   83
59. Memories-12/14/21   84
60. Pumpkins-9-29-21   85
61. The Bluebonnets-4/22/21   86
62. April Again-4/4/22   87
63. A New Beginning-7/14/22   88

II. B. Poems by Michael Autry

64. Rhythm   90
65. Brother   91
66. Bridges   93
67. Masculine   95
68. Sunblind   97
69. Sunskin, Moonheart, Hailmind   98
70. To Stop and Go   100
71. Friend   102
72. A Soft Ache, This Hounding Agitation   103
73. Song Bird   105
74. Tall Tales   107
75. Tired   109
76. Justify Me Ye Space   110
77. Peace   112
78. This Holy Fire   113
79. You're Elemental Necessity, Our Garden's Need   114
80. Of Two Minds and Many, End with Enmity for Any Remedy   116
81. Thank You   118
82. O Ignis Caritatis   119
83. Angels   121
84. Desire   123
85. Resist   124
86. What Might Be   125
87. An Epiphany   126
88. You   127

III. Afterword by Bruce C. Autry

89. Love's Fool   129

I. Bruce C. Autry

Sonnets

1. My Celtic Girl

A lovely Celtic girl with reddish hair,
And rusty freckles spread through milky skin,
This daughter, Irish bred, beyond compare,
A Gaelic siren song of love again,
O Babes, if you and I in times to come,
In other worlds of heaven's embrace hide
From times of fife and pounding ancient drum,
With wings of wizard power we decide
To rise through clouds of angry icy storm
To find a world beyond those who deride
Our subtle glances of tender affection
Let us escape from those attempts to numb
Our throbbing hearts in need of reflection
To stave off those who compel us to conform.

2. Real Estate

Through sunny Denver I in silence walk
Around a place of shelter for the old
And noting small and peaceful untold
And forgotten moments of graceful talk,
My heart does not refrain nor balk
From encounters with your memory sold
For neither lost time nor borrowed gold
Listed in some abandoned boardroom's chalk.
Here I may through buying and selling cash
The thousand promissory notes you signed
With indelible ink upon the lawyer's deed,
So may I reap where others clash
And find a treasure trove so refined
That neither heart no soul shall ever bleed.

3. Mexican Smoke

A sunless day of Mexican smoke,
The heat a foretaste of hell.
Come to me, on sweet Death.
Let ring the iron funeral bell
As now I choke
And lose my last, lonely breath.
The half-empty glass of all my days,
Broken promises that litter my mind,
Debris from the summer's spree,
And still I remember her ways,
A cast-off melon's half-eaten rind
And her desire to be free.
Take me for what I am:
No hero now, just a sham.

4. Remember the Alamo

O glorious Celtic hearts that bled this day,
I pause to honor you on bended knee.
My Celtic ring reflects the glory of your loss,
And your deaths this day we all should agree
Saved us from the yoke of foreign decree.
O fearless Celtic brothers whose cross
I wear in the light of this late winter day
I honor you and mourn your bloody gashes.
Be it ever remembered that your ashes
Rest beneath the live oaks covered with moss.
Though a thousand years may come to this earth
What you did this day made possible a new birth
And our Celtic hearts shall proclaim your worth
O glorious and free this day and all eternity.

5. The Last Lament

My Celtic cross fell from her neck
As the waves battered the shipwreck.
The broken chain could not hold
And her secret heart would never
Feel the caress of my cold
Hand in the deepest winter's embrace.
For the words "Friends Forever"
Now left not a single trace.
The mermaid faded into a wave
Where no sun would warm
Her little tattoo, the white heart,
A twin of my phantom's form,
While the lonely gulls cried for my lost art.

6. Somewhere in Time

In time she hides
A frozen rose,
A red fragment of a dream
In the ruins of a heart
Too soon bruised by day
And broken by night.
In time she glides
Through the silky rustle
Of drawing rooms
Where spring forever blooms
And tides of Arabian perfume
In a swirling misty scene
Touch the fiber of her soul
Upon the warp of time.

7. The Winds of Skye

Oh, Isle of Skye where my grandfathers lie,
Oh, Isle of Skye, there my body too will die.
Your winds forever blow through northern air
Your winds forever grow through nature's care.
Oh, the winds blow hard on the Isle of Skye.
Even gods cry for a woman who loved a prince.
Oh, Flora, oh, Flora, where you still lie,
In the sacred ground of Skye where starlings fly
Oh, blow, north wind, through the Highlands.
Oh, blow from the heavens the stormy gale.
Blow, you old north wind of the lonely islands,
As when the disguised heir with nary a pence
Evaded his enemies to put the Skye boat to sail
Past the Jacobites lying beneath a Scottish sky.

8. A Gentle Rain

I like to walk in a gentle rain;
It cleanses my heart of all its pain,
And I can remember the joy
We shared once upon a time
As the fairy tales often begin
But who knows how the ploy
Of seeking to find a rhyme
May turn my smiles to chagrin?
I like to talk in a simple refrain
Of how the memory of all our days
Even now a year later can sustain
My trembling hands as they gain
The answer to the depth of your gaze
In my wandering in this final haze.

9. Ungifted Gift

I have always loved to receive gifts,
But one gift I wanted to give to you
Never came to pass, my Celtic lass.
I have always striven to mend the rifts,
But one rift I failed to tend anew.
I cannot let this toxic omission pass,
For my mind, seeking heavenly remission, shifts
From worldly devotion to the Holy Mass.
Oh, how I wanted you to have Paris
In the spring with the avenues
Adorned with bouquets and your eyes
Wandering from the Mona Lisa to the Kiss!
Knowing that all of this beauty that we pursue
Will forever endure in other lovers' sighs.

10. My Green Beret

My brother Al was a Green Beret;
Am I the only one who remembers?
He was infantry, then Ranger reserve;
And then the army chose his last seque
Through the Special Forces where
He heard his country's call, but did not fall
And end up with his name upon the wall.
Am I only one who remembers?
He looked sharp in his dress uniform.
He spent his summer vacation standing tall
Or sheltering in place from July storms.
Am I the only one who remembers?
Even I can't find his old headwear
Leaving me only his memories to preserve.

11. My Three Brothers

When I think of my three brothers,
All older and all gone,
I wonder if I like the dawn
Will break as all the others
Or has the dealer stacked the deck
With cards foretelling some fatal wreck?
Or will secret gas that smothers
Fill my room like water drawn
From the ancient Isle of Skye fairy pools
Where two lovers may fool
Themselves with promises better not made
If the death card must be played?
Shuffle the cards for one last hand
As the one behind the mask will command.

12. The Woman That I Loved

She died in this room,
The woman that I loved.
She died in her sleep,
This woman, my bride
Who made me her groom.
The woman I loved who died
Her body lay ringed not gloved
And in the ocean so deep,
We set adrift a portion
Of her ashes we could not keep
And like some modern Houdini,
I felt the contortion
Of my heart's sorrowful debris,
All that remains of her in me.

13. Too Late

I went to the mountains too late;
My time had passed,
No, you still have a date,
Some may say,
For you will surely last.
No, I will not lay
Down my feeble fears
While I cannot pray
To undo the damage of my years,
So let us agree to disagree
You say that I still have a lease,
But I say I have my release;
You say that's not the way to calculate;
But I say that's the way to conflate.

Free Verse

14. Flora's Dream

Will my lord , my future king, ever come to this,
My little Scottish home among the Highlands?
I've been waiting to hear his voice,
To throw my arms about his neck.
When I smell the air fresh and clean,
When I hear the wind over the hills,
When I see the white roses growing,
When I feel the chilly rain upon my face,
When I taste the warm haggis on my tongue,
I know he will be my lord, my king.
Prince Charlie, the Stuart of my dreams,
Come, O come to me here among my Highlands.
I'll nurse your wounds, I'll kiss your cheeks
When you come to this my Highland home.
When will you let me dance the fling for you
Where the white roses bloom among the stones?
There will I wait until you come, my lord,
My king, my bonnie lad who will be my king.
I'll wear the white rose of the Jacobites
In my hair and festoon my gown with petals.
The white rose of Scotland I'll wear for you
All the days of my life in my brown hair.
I'll pin a rose to my dreams and let you
Nestle safely there at one with me and God.

15. Flora's Fling

Let me dance, oh, let me dance for you,
Let me dance, oh, let me dance as I used to do.
I will fling away your cares,
I will sing away your cares.
Oh, let me dance for you!

16. The Tower

Oh, Lord, my King, how have I failed you?
This tower, this prison is nothing to my soul.
I roam the Highlands here on English soil
Neither contained nor restrained by these stones.
I have stood where Anne Bolyne lost her head
And did I lose mine for Bonnie Prince Charlie?
I told the Duke of Cumberland
That I would have saved him if he
Had come to me as Bonnie Prince Charlie did.
Did I lie to him or to myself?
If I must die in this English prison,
My soul will not haunt these stones.
My blood is Scottish blood,
My rose is the white rose
I will fly upon the wind to the Isle
Of Skye where my fathers lie.
No English charms will hold me here.
I have not failed in my love, oh, my King,
I serve a righteous God who redeems.
Oh, my king, my heavenly king on earth,
You have failed, oh, you have failed us!
But I will dress you now, a servant of us all,
And guide you to the freedom land
Across the Irish sea. Remember me!

17. Flora's Grave

A white rose still grows
On Flora's grave.
Bonny Prince Charlie
Gave her the rose.
You could not see it then,
For it was only in his mind,
But now, look at the roses bloom.
The wild rose still grows
Underneath a Scottish sky
Where Flora lies.
Bow your heads and kneel upon the ground.
Sing sad songs of him who lost the crown,
A bonnie lad, fearless soul, who fought for us.
Oh, God, oh God, lift him up to your gates
Open wide, open wide, and let him hide
In the blessed bosom of you, God.
Open wide, open wide those heavenly gates.
Open wide, open wide the heavenly sky.
Dressed as a woman let him sail away
Dressed as a servant let him sail away.

18. A Winged Fortune Cookie

I had never seen a magpie in the wild
Until one morning at Steamboat Springs,
I saw a flock apparently feeding near me.
Then a few weeks later on a snowy day
They shook the branches of their favorite tree
Sending a shower of snow falling
To the snow-covered ground.
They repeated this activity as though they
Were a fly crew clearing their landing zones
Or playing a game to pass the time.
Then this summer in Denver
In the midst of summer on a morning walk,
I spied a flock of magpies exploring the grounds
Of the dementia center near my apartment.
They pecked in the lush green grass
And then fluttered to the limbs of the fir trees.
They did not chatter nor commune with me.
They did not even notice me, nor the small
Rabbit exploring the same grounds as we.
I wonder how these messengers
From the creator and the guardians of the East
Earned their reputation from the Cheyenne,

The Hopi, and the Pueblo.
I did not understand their messages,
If any or what they guarded,
But I did know they caught
My eye if not my ear
And this I took for my good luck
As the Chinese and the Koreans do,
And yet there must be a dark side.
My Scottish blood did not burn
Hotter learning that my ancestors
Saw a drop of devil's blood
Upon the magpie's tongue
Or that the Scandinavians
Charged the birds with being a sign
Of witches and the Germans assigned
Them to the depths of the Underworld.
No, I saw a group moving
With an intense purpose,
But I did not know then that these birds
Were known for violence against the eggs
And fledglings of other innocent songbirds.
Then I learned that they become aggressive
When humans approach their nests.
I read of an Australian mother
Who lost her five-month-old daughter
When aggressive magpies caused the mother
To lose her balance and her baby

Fell to her death.
A good news message of luck
From the creator seems lost
Among the blades of green grass,
And I have not seen the magpies
Since my ramble on a sunny summer morning
With nothing on my mind but a hydrating drink,
But still I wonder how different
Are they from us.

19. The Comfort of Quilts

I remember the sound of the rain
On winter mornings
When I lay beneath a bundle
Of homemade quilts.
The outer cold announcing its presence
More powerfully than any clock
Could not persuade me to rise
And leave the comfort
Of those sheltering patches
Where five more minutes
Charmed me with the illusion
Of peace and good will.

20. When You Leave

When you leave, I shall cry
Such tears as fell from Adam's eyes
Upon the corpse of Abel.
When you leave, I shall lie
As weary as Sisyphus's heart
Viewing the stone roll back again.
When you leave, I shall heave
Such sighs as rose from Eve
When the gates of Paradise closed
Upon the naked fragments of her soul.
Call this love? Be it so, when
Two hearts roll around the heavens
Like two wandering stars,
Vagabonds of the open road,
Seeking that moment of gravity
That draws them down upon themselves
To form the final black hole.
O twin of my tattered flag,
When you leave, I shall cry
Such sounds that rose from Mary
When the Son of Man breathed his last.

21. The Phantom's Death

The music of the night.
No longer beckons me to the hall.
Her voice has silenced the tenor
Of my days, and the nights
Now sing no arias to my soul.
Somewhere in time my heart
Is floating tonight, somewhere
In time, somewhere, I wander
In time, somewhere tonight.

22. The Rose of All Time

I brought a single rose
From heaven knows
Where to adorn her hair
And a ring,
A priceless thing
To circle her finger.
Now I linger
To hear her sing,
My rose of all Time,
My Angel, Christine.

23. Change

There in the hushed stillness
Of her darkened room
In the quiet recesses
Of her gentle mind,
He came to her now
With the eternity of her need,
A moment of tenderness
To share in a room
No longer adjoining.

24. Foretaste of Hell

What they share now
Is only the fragments of a vow.
Words uttered before a priest
Through the years have ceased
To convey a remnant of love
Torn and scattered above
The scarred, charred ruins
Of the pain in the loins.

25. Liar's Club

If you come to Texas,
I will meet you there.
If you come to Texas,
I will bring you yellow ribbons
For your auburn hair.
If you come to Texas,
I will greet you there.
If you come to Texas,
I will sing you a ballad
To show you how much I care.

26. Lost in Time

In another time, another day,
I might have loved you well,
But we live in the now,
And I can't touch you,
I can't reach you,
So let the sun go down
Upon our love.

27. The Gift

I found a blue and golden book,
Musty and dark on a metal shelf
Bathed in soft fluorescent light.
The book, an aged romance of wigwam and
cabin,
Seemed an old thing of paper, glue, and ink
'Til I opened the fragile boards
And saw in faded brown a hand
From beyond the grave whose smooth strokes
Told of parental love now dead
Like the knell of the village bell.
I held the dead man's book, the boy
Who pored over these pages when new,
Long dead and gone, extinguished like the old
people
Of the big wood who chased the deer and bear
'Til the Great Spirit called out of the whirlwind,
The mournful wail of death.
I held the dead man's book, the boy
Who chased his dream in the shimmer
And shine, twisting shadow dancing
Fire of the cool October sky,
Long dead and gone in the eddy of fading time,
I held the dead man's book, the boy,

Who gifted me a glimpse of myself
Through a path leading across time and space
To the brink of all things past, all things future
Here through the faded hand, the silent
Voice still audible above the din of modern guns
And bombs and midnight assassins crouched by
the baby's door.
The dead love still blooms in the swirl
Of these old letters from the grave.

28. Books and Other Oddities of Love

I like the smell of new books
Saturating my porous mind
With a green stream whose branches
Will redeem my sinful will.

I like the sound of a pencil
Scratching its cryptic code
Upon a white page whose acid
Will consume the bitter fruit.

I like the look of the sea
Bathing the littered beach
With a white-capped wave whose salt
Will cleanse the deepest wound.

I like the taste of old love
Sweetening my yellow days
With the candied past whose sugar
Will regale my slender soul.

I like the feel of her skin
Warming my calloused hand

With an autumnal promise whose power
Will repair my broken heart.

29. The Walker

I see her almost everyday
Walking her laps with the aid
Of a modern contraption
Around the assisted-living facility.
Sometimes she pauses to adjust
Her mask or to pick up
A yellow flower or touch a hedge.
I wonder what she thinks
Of those wild-eyed maniacs
Who shun what she embraces.
Who is free and who is the slave?
I wonder if I will do so well
When my old legs will lose their balance.
Will I have the courage to circle
The neighborhood without a companion,
Not even a pet to share the journey?
I wonder and I admire the life
She possesses after so many silent laps
Around a sun that will one day expire.
I wonder if my inner voice
That has been my comforter
Will be enough on late sunny days
To keep me moving forward
Like a marathoner on the final mile

Of what has been an incredible run.
Yes, I wonder, oh, I do, indeed, wonder
If I will do so well when my final days
To circle this little piece of earth will come.
I wonder if someone might pause
And say: "Look at him go, look at him go."

30. My Paternal Grandmother

I have seen her only in one picture
Taken sometime around nineteen-fifteen,
A family portrait formal to suit the times.
She looks like Willa Cather, the writer,
Wearing the same masculine necktie,
Seated next to her husband,
My grandfather who looks like
He stepped off the stage in the Old West.
I wonder what Grandma's voice
Would have sounded like calling me
To a supper I never ate on a farm
I never knew in those old days.
Her father had been a hellfire preacher
Who married twice and sired twenty-two
Children, one of whom wounded
At Gettysburg limped for the rest of his life.
I doubt Grandma would approve of me
With my modern liberal manners and ideas,
Untutored in her ways of picking cotton
Or curing tobacco or killing hogs.
She died more than a decade
Before I was born on a farm,

A place which I know only from its ruins.
If could share one word with Grandma,
It would be *faith,* for without that
I might as well hang up my book bag
And slither away like a reptile in the grass.

31. My Maternal Grandmother

I have only one personal memory
Of Grandma Black, but I have seen her
In several old black and white photographs.
In each she is holding a grandchild or Bible.
My one personal memory comes from a visit
Grandma made to see my family when I was
Three or four years old. My mother bought
Extra cereal at the store for my grandparents.
I remember that Grandma's voice was soft
And sweet, and she called my mother "Betty,"
As they chatted as two women in our kitchen.
The one present that Grandma bought for me
Was a small plastic bow with a couple
Of rubber-tipped arrows causing no harm.
I also remember a little baby quilt
She made for my sister, covered with little
Fishes, and my envious heart wondered
If Grandma had made me a patchwork quilt
When I was a baby and my mother assured me
That she had surely not left this little rascal out.
One other story that my mother shared with me
Was of the triplet boys that Grandma had who

Weighed so little that they did not survive.
They did not receive names but filled one grave.
Many years later they were exhumed
And reburied in a new plot somewhere
Unknown to me as so much family life
Remains shrouded in the dim light of the past.
Now as an old man, I see archetypal images
In these fading pictures of that long ago time:
Images of motherhood, the home, the church.
Life was hard and often unfair, but families
Had each other and the fellowship of the church
And the old-time religion and that faith, yes,
That same faith that connects me to my father's
Mother connects me as well to my mother's
mother and that faith carried them
Through time and tide, as surely as it carries me
now in my final days.

32. My Paternal Grandfather

In the one photograph of my paternal
grandfather,
He looks like a replica of Wyatt Earp,
With his hat off and thick mustache, a hero
Sitting with his wife and children in the fashion
Of smile-less faces. The three children dressed
In their best stare off in their chosen directions
As though they were not posing at all, each lost
In thought. Grandpa Autry was not a gunslinger,
Nor marshal from the streets of Tombstone nor
Dodge City, or a player at the OK Corral.
The structure in the background is not
An old saloon, but a weather-beaten farmhouse,
Not a mansion, though slaves of some plantation
Owner may have labored to bring order out of
A pile of boards. The only gun associated
With Grandpa was a single-barreled shotgun
That my father retained as his only heirloom.
When the circle of life spun round to my time,
I refused my inheritance as I am not a hunter
Of small game, though my sins do include
Killing one snowbird.

I wonder now what Grandpa would have thought
of me;
We of the present so often judge the past as if
Those of those old times were as familiar
To us as our jeans.
I wonder now what those old folks would say
Of us who have never treed a coon at midnight
Nor stretched a hide upon a barn door.
Grandpa, would you have used your fists to set
Me straight? My mother spoke highly of your
Twinkling blue eyes,
So just maybe, you would have cut this ole boy
Some slack.
Grandpa, I carry your genes, and maybe
I stand tall
Because of those hidden markers giving me
Blue eyes.
Grandpa, I sign a pact with you today one Autry
To another to cherish the land and all that grows
And to cut you some slack as you would do me;
For as long as the wind blows and the snows
Fall upon this good earth, I will wonder and
pray that we will stand shoulder to shoulder
In the heaven to come, for we can never go
back.

33. My Maternal Grandfather

I owe you an apology for being a mocking child,
Who let having fun at your expense eclipse
My duty to share a Christian charity
For your dementia, a disease I did not know.
I think the silliness of my fixation upon comedy
Was greater than my understanding of mortality,
So the ravages of old age upon your memory
Became a game of "Who am I, Grandpa?"
And I knew your answer would be incorrect,
But my laughter at your mistake has not
Diminished its damage to my memories of you,
For it was I who was wrong to the nth degree,
So my ability to mimic your shuffle from room
To room was no remarkable feat, but a callous
Indiscretion unbecoming of a child taught
The Christian virtues by his mother.
Schooled in Old Testament vengeance, I thought
My own shuffle brought on by my appendicitis,
Was God's curse upon me, and I was ashamed.
I remember how your one pleasure was bubble
Gum, the kind that came one stick to a football
Card during the fall when baseball was over.

You chewed the gum and gave me the cards,
So I had the eleven cards of the starting
Offense for the glorious Baltimore Colts
Led by Johnny Unitas and his favorite
Target, Raymond Berry. You had no
Idea who they were, but you gave the cards
Knowing that those little pieces of paper
Were prized more by me than the pieces
Of paper called money adorned with faces
Of Washington and Lincoln who had not
Become icons in my pantheon of greats,
For they played neither football nor baseball.
Yes, Grandfather, I have much to confess and
Much to thank you for, as in these my own last
Days, I never get to see my grandchildren, so
In the zero-sum gamesmanship of today,
What I took from you did not add to my pile
Of chips, but reduced my pot of gold to dust.
Forgive me, Grandfather, for I have sinned;
This is my first confession since you departed
This life; let these days of penance restore
My soul before I meet you in heaven
With all the angels and saints.

34. Dead Bird

I saw a dead bird today;
A magpie or a starling,
Which it was I could not say;
A pile of Starbucks' cups
Littered the concrete where it lay.
Alone it was no one's darling,
So morbid thoughts I had to give up
For it was time to be on my way.

35. Femme Fatale

O how I did love the lies
That fell from her magic lips,
Words of her inner circle,
Her heart's deep core;
O how I let my reason
Unbridled rush over her cliff
And then I awoke to her crimson fangs
Pumping their poison into my neck.

And like the bruised and battered king
Who from Agincourt's muddy earth
Did lift his eyes to heaven I cried:
"O God of Wisdom steel my heart to her lies
Let me resist the death
Nestled between her thighs.

I will chant a thousand Hail Marys
And do penance upon the narrowest streets
If that will break the demon's spell.

Cleanse me now of the murderous stain
Of her name, the polluted memory of her deadly
touch.
Erase from my lips the foul remnants
Of her vampire's kiss.

Let not one fevered memory,
Not one scarlet delusion,
Not one bloody illusion
Color me with the disease of her beauty.
Let me rise once more
To bless this good earth and blow
The final trumpet's charge into love's embrace.

36. Twilight Love

Each night she spins her cocoon,
A silken Wall of China,
A Maginot Line,
Beyond which I cannot go.
She imprisons herself in her tower
And I, not Lancelot,
Not Galahad,
Not even Prufrock,
I cannot flash my sword
Or burnish my armor in the noon-day sun
To catch her eyes,
Nor in the dazzling moonlight
Where wild roses should bloom
In her hair

She sleeps
Locked in her own self-made world,
A tangle of orders and retreats.
No tricky weaver deceiving her suitors,
She has closed her elfin grot
And I neither knight nor king
Neither prophet nor shaman,
I—I—I—curse my withered heart,
Blanched and blotched,
Brittle and besmirched

Wandering and wondering
Why the mockingbird's song
Calls me back to the scene of my defeat.

37. In Memoriam: Karla Faye Tucker

What must you have been
Thinking
On your final day.
I thought of you
Often
As the minutes ticked down,
And yet I knew you
Only
As a face beamed through space
By the technocrats of our age,
The media
Who feed
Upon our souls
Until we are just the carrion
For the scavengers
Of this lurid time.
How dare the state
Take what God
Had given you,
Even if in your fatal youth
You mistook the drugs
And the violence
As a way

To ease your pain.
You have gone to be with the Lord,
But, Angel,
You were with the Lord
Long before
The State of Texas
In justice's name
Took
The holy gift of life
That only God should take.
Yes, Karla, you have seen the Lord,
And in your angelic face
We have seen Him too.
God bless you
In your eternal embrace
In the bosom of our Holy Savior,
Jesus Christ.
Amen,
Amen.

38. The Waterfall

In a foreign land shrouded with the mists
Of time, the eternal waters pour over the cliffs
And remind me of my own raging dreams
And sunless days of bitter, forlorn intent
And shake my soul with the chilling   reminder
Of what might have been in the summer
Of some lost year when you, wild demon of
The heartland, stole my power and left me
Bruised, battered, broken upon this desert.
My waterfall disappeared amid the bursting
Bombs of that lost time when I fooled myself
Thinking a surprise attack upon my heart
Would not leave my romantic soul in shreds
And falling tears my only fall of water.

39. Heavenly Justice

When I go down to the darkness,
I will see the light of your angelic face,
Just compensation for the trials
Of this our long separation.
Justice requires a readjustment
Of the tally book or else there is no God.
In spite of your suffering,
All your questioning of what the fate
Of your brain would be,
You could still smile and hold my hand.
O, my darling Babes, we two shared a love
Tossed and battered by the sea's cold waves,
But still we never quit our stroking toward the
shore.
You have reached the other side where you
bathe
In the sun's holy light and I pine on the earthly
beach
Drenched by the loneliness of this mortal life,
And still you come back to me in my desire
In the hours of my quiet need to return to the sea
Where my stroking will propel me to the light
Where you wait to wrap me in the drying robes
Of your saintly love timeless beyond this sea

Of human time that too must end with a
whimper.

40. Ripe Cherries

When the cherries are ripe in the Rockies,
I'll be back in the saddle again,
Without apologies to Cousin Gene
Who had no interest in genealogies
For too many distant cousins
Tried to hit him up for some of his bucks.
I can see the resemblance to him
Of my first cousin but not so much
In my own aging face,
So let the cherries ripen and I will
Declare only blood kin and lament
That I came too late to watch Gene
In the first run of his movies,
But they still hold up against time,
And Champion still runs the desert
As fast as any horse that ever galloped
Across the silver screen and into the hearts
Of the millions and millions of kids who
Wished with all their might that they too
Could saddle up and ride with Gene
To the mountains where the cherries ripen.

41. Masks

On my ramble through my neighborhood,
I saw a pandemic mask, blue and white,
Hanging from a green hedge.
Was this a joke by a second-rate comic
Or a protest against government mandates?
I wear my own mask like a Greek actor
In a tragedy by ancient Sophocles
Hoping to shield myself from the virus,
Yet knowing that indifferent fate
Has more in store for me
Than I can fathom or ignore,
And still I wonder who marked
My walking trail with a sign
Or symbol of what yet may be.

42. Seasonal Magic

Every season has its magic.
Spring dresses the countryside
In blues and yellows and reds.
Summer warms our bodies
With its golden rays
And tans our skin.
Fall brings out the red and orange
Leaves transforming nature's pallet
Into an array of paints,
Each scene an impression
Of the Great Creator's love of diversity.
Winter's snow, the purest white,
Cleanses an ordinary day
Leaving sculptures upon the living earth.
I cannot say one is my favorite,
For each touches my mind
Altering what could have been a regret
And making me happy to be alive.
So this must be magic.

43. Choices; For the Season of Lent

I am saddened when I choose a book,
For to choose is to reject the many,
But when we find our love we are not sad.
And yet I think each choice is not so much
A victory as a defeat; she who chose me
Defeated the loneliness at my core
And slew the dragons who plagued my soul.
Now I put the book back upon its shelf
Needing not to read another page,
For she who chose me wrote the Book of Life
That I hear in her voice beyond the grave.
And her poetry is not of this place and time,
But comes to me in fantastic sleep,
A harbinger of the new edition to come.

44. Let It Go

From the second-story window of my room,
I saw two rabbits in the snow,
And I thought how much like human lovers
They were, spending the winter afternoon
Together bundled in their winter coats.
I finished my lime-mint tea for the moment
Content that the evil overseas is something
They would never know and for a few seconds
I did not shiver as I remembered the song
Of the Ukrainian girl in the shelter who sang
"Let It Go" with a purity and innocence that
 Putin will never know hiding in the Kremlin.

45. Pieces

Pieces of my broken heart are scattered
Over the grounds I can visit only in memory,
But know that I visit there in the rain
Like a homeless kitten searching for a place
To curl in midnight sleep that does not come.

46. Mule Deer

I saw what at first appeared to be a mule,
And then I stared until I could make out a doe
Nibbling leaves from a tree
In my neighbor's yard.
She soon bedded down in the shade and flipped
Her tail, though I did not see any flies, the cool
Spring air with the ground patched
With late snow.
I wondered if she might be with foal
Soon to be born in this early spring.
Would she bring her fawn back for me to see?
This natural give lifted my spirit
As I forgot my troubles
And stared at her huge ears visible in the shade.
For a moment peace ruled my heart and I forgot
About the terrible wars raging
Beyond Castle Rock wishing that world leaders
Could know the peace of this spring day,
A birthday gift to surpass
All other prescriptions in our time.

47. Castle Rock

I have become a high-plains drifter
Watching the snow fall without regard
To the calendar's seasonal labels.
Castle Rock does not brood over me.
 It proudly waves its flag through days
Of sunshine as the wind blows
As though the air must be on the move
Like a restless traveler from another time.
I long to climb to the very top where
I would open my arms to embrace
The world and pray a thanksgiving hymn
Acknowledging Him who made this Eden
And let my soul soar like the lonesome dove
Bringing the olive branch to the scattered flock.

48. The Gothic Bookshop

I spent hours and dollars
Pouring over the best collections
Of literary history and criticism
In any bookshop I have ever encountered
Lost in my mind of weighing and touching
Until my desire to possess exceeded my budget.
Isn't that the way of a scholar whose naiveté
Assumes an intellectual kinship with the dead
That cannot exorcise the demons of discipleship,
So the miles I walked in circles sifting,
Hefting the sacred tomes only weighed
Down my spirit and would not free me?
Is this what makes a bibliophile,
This worship of the printed word,
This voyage through others' seas
Until our baptism drowns our own souls
In the holy water blessed by the shamans
And I come back from my pilgrimage
And kneel to search the lowest shelf
In silent meditation until the mantra
Spirals invisibly from my nostrils
Like the incense in a devotee's chapel

And I know not where to crouch
In nook or cranny until the end comes.

49. Parkinson's

It is cold here
Where the shadow of death
Covers me like a patchwork quilt
But I do not shiver in vain,
For I have fought off panic
And lie down to dreams
Filled with hallucinations,
Harbingers of the tremors,
A foretaste of the Parkinson's
That abides near me
Like a faithful valet.

50. Viva La Vida

Blind men see more than we,
So don't let your pity
Run down your face
In streaks of crimson
Now fully out of place.
Why cry drops of blood
For those who cannot see
Leaving not a single trace
Of that remembered day
Which took your breath away?
Turn back upon your own
Shattered heart and shed
The last shards of hidden bone
And celebrate one last kiss
For nothing can replace the bliss
Of that hour in the splendid sun,
That eternity paid in the golden spangles
Of holy light cataracts could not hide.
Oh, let the arias soar through the darkness
And forgive my foolish tears
That nothing now may I dread,
Free falling from the mountaintop.

51. The Old Home Place

I ramble through time
Back to the old home place,
Which still stands against the winds
Even though the giant oak met its doom
When Hurricane Andrew blew it
Down upon the roof
Tearing a hole in it
Much like a hole in my heart.

I can still see the poplar and the maple
My father planted
Growing together though the maple
Has not been pruned
In years and has muscled its way
Through the poplar's space
Spreading its red branches
Like a cancerous string.

The hedge that captured
So many of our baseballs
Has met the chopper's blade and hides
Nothing now.
The china berries and pecans murdered by hands
Unknown

Have filled the trash trucks and tempt no more
climbers.

It is time to ramble no more; it is time to go,
So I leave,
Not in peace, but of a piece,
Of a wrinkle in time,
Folded like a tattered flag that will fly no more.
Let "Taps" play as I fade slowly away,
Solemnly away
And leave the old home place
To lie in nature's arms.

52. Risqué

How short must it be
Below the heart
But above the knee?
Where does it start
To tell the story?

II. The Autry Siblings

A. Margaret Autry

53. Good Morning

Fall 2018

You ask me how I'm doing.
I hide the truths as I answer
Okay with what...
Okay with the world flipping upside down.
I thought gravity was my friend
And love always sets us free.
Free from reality and the sins I can't take back.
Where is my friend? Where is my love?
To the clouds I release
My silent scream.
Look up.
Answer.
I'm okay, how are you?

54. FML 8/20/20

I'm trying so hard but I'm still drowning.
Just when I feel afloat, the current sweeps me
under.
The waves engulf my lungs.
As I'm pushed ashore
I cough out my insecurities and fall upon the
sand.
I wheeze and feel the sun warm my inspirations.
I'll do it all over again tomorrow.

55. Untitled 12-24-20

The tree is lit but my heart is dim.

I stretch my arm out in hope to feel your strength.
But I'm left with the quiet of the thin air.

I listen to the carols in hope to feel you singing.
But I'm left with the loneliness of the melodies.

I drop to my knees and look to the heavens
in hope for the love of God.
But I'm left with the echoes of my prayers.

56. Hope 6/26/21

I look around and see the smiles
I see the laughter that fills their void
It used to bring pain to my stomach
To my heart to my memories.

I look around and see the world change
I see the cars drive past
It used to bring me to exhaustion to my legs
To my heart to my memories.

I look around feel myself put one foot
in front of the other
I see myself living among these people that
Used to bring me pain to my knees
To my heart to my memories.

I look around and smile for the hope of my
Future.

57. Lucky 7/2/21

I used to think I had the worst luck.

Last in line
Red light every time.
Dropped food in the kitchen
Second in the competition.
No more unicorn frap
Charged again for that free app.
Stole my joke
Look at my cracked yolk.
Best friend gone to heaven
Closed the seven eleven.

But I just received a lesson
That I couldn't have been guessin'.

His love is not like most.
He gives me what I hoped.
How lucky am I?

58. Can I take a trip to Heaven? 11-11-21

Can I take a trip to heaven today?
I promise it will just take a minute.
I can walk my way and knock upon the door
As long as you will answer.

Can I take a trip to heaven today?
I promise to embrace the beauty.
I can walk among the flowers and not a take a
picture.
As long as you will hug me once more.

Can I take a trip to heaven today?
I promise to appreciate the time.
I can walk my way back and hold my head high.
As long as I can get the strength from you.

Can I take a trip to heaven today?
I promise it will just take one minute.

59. Memories 12-14-21

You flip through an album
But I scroll through the voicemails.
Just to hear one more time the voice.
Why didn't I answer that day?
What could I have been doing that was ever so
important?
At the time it didn't seem to matter
But now it's all I have left.
You only you.
One last time… okay call me back.

60. Pumpkins 9/29/21

Fall is here and pumpkins are near.
I remember you cutting the pumpkin top so I
could grab its insides.
The guts would ooze between my fingers as I
squeezed my palms.
My giggles brought joy to your face.
Rinse the seeds you said
so I can cook'em for you.

Fall is here and pumpkins are near.
I remember selecting the tiny ones to add to your
centerpiece.
Light the candles and fill the bowl.
It's my turn to be a big kid even though my
Innocence was not yet take from me.
Who trick or treats at 16?

Fall is here and pumpkins are near.
I now select the newest pumpkin late in hope
to bring back my childhood joy.

Fall is here and pumpkins are near.
Pumpkins which were ever so lovely
are every so lonely.

61. The Bluebonnets 4-22-21

It's that time of year again
when April showers bring May flowers.

But it's different this year.
As I look at the bluebonnets
It's as if I'm seeing the memories through a lens.

I see my pink converse and scuffed knees.
I see the endless winding roads
I see the Texas sunset.
But what I see most is your smile.

As I look at the bluebonnets
I see you, Mom and smile.

62. April again... 4-4-22

The bluebonnets are back.
I drive past as the worries of the day fill my brain.
Racing cars, racing thoughts.

Why can't I appreciate their beauty today.
I know I need to feel the memories
Of that green house on Allegria.
With a bird bath in the corner.
And pine trees as tall as the wind.
And a swing set I used as a jungle gym.
The backyard was a field to me
But now it's just a patch of old green.

Who lives in that house now among our
memories?
The memories that I hold so dear to my heart
That not one could tear them apart.

You may not see the bluebonnets but to me
They are my everything.

63. A New Beginning 7-14-22

Walking through what has felt like the fires of
Hell
The grass is no longer green but patches of brown.
The flowers have wilted in the shadows of the
willow trees.
The rivers have run dry among the burning sun.
But what is this among the heat.
A bluebonnet is blooming in a room full of
strangers.
Its growth dependent upon a soul who was once
lost.
And just like that the Heavens bless its beauty
With the tears of all the angels.
Let these tears soak the Earth to flourish the
beauty that was ever so lost.

B. Michael Autry

64. Rhythm

Life in rhythm?
That's a dance.
And dance is really just music.
And music is poetry.
And language?
That's a symbol.
But symbols in form?
That's art.
And art in rhythm?
That's life.

65. Brother

His face is here but eyes there.
A stare as blank as blackboard.
I could write it red with my hate.
Dusty white hides pale green,
The boards in this building are older, not in
years, but in wisdom.
They smell of distant memories, still whispering
tales of pleasurable insights through
lungs, deeper still, embedded in my strongest
muscle. Heart beats on and on and on,
but softer and softer. I can hear it only in quiet
moments of slipping mind. Always to
swing around. Always centered. Always.
He directs his pain into hatred of others. My
brother! What's happened to you? I can't
stand next to you. I won't defend you. I take
chalk and mark your mind with my
experience, but someone's greasy hand, dripping
with insidious deception, has
smeared it into blindness oblivion. Your mind is
behind. Eyes won't see. I can't speak
to you when ears won't listen. I miss you, my
brother. I wish so much to give you but
one taste of the peace I've found. Only a piece

even I hold, always focused on finding
the others. I know you hurt as I do. Please,
brother, make peace with this world. It's not
against you!

66. Bridges

We *should* build bridges, not walls. When a wall blocks the mind it might still be crossed, but with how much difficulty? We must devise plans to scale its unknown heights, or burrow deep below its sinking roots to squirm on belly slowly though dank darkness of red-brown clay. But bridges over river-split minds, will provide. Any may cross at their own pace. Some wildly spring, endlessly open. Others stay steady, though their speeds may vary. I look to the side and the river distracts my eye. It's pattern of flow, this rushing gush of ever-changing water. I peer beyond the blue dark and see but a wisp of something thrashing in the current. I turn it around in my mind looking for its form, its answer. I've lost sight of the others. Some stumble and fall, they look back and wonder if they should cross at all. I must call out to set them right, "Look forward, friends!" But my words are weak. I wish someone else to speak, Until voice is found. I stay steady now. At times I glance to the river below, "How deep are your waters? How long and many these bridges? Are they wide enough for us all?

How many will pass by and never cross at all? Should I mind this conundrum, the running river always undone?" No. Keep eyes fixed on the distant dot, and fill your periphery with every bridge you've sought.

67. Masculine

I grew upon around a bunch of women. I have a bit of the feminine. Three sisters, one mother, all, and another, strong personalities always guiding me. And the other? Yes a man, but not always like that. He couldn't fix shit, but still told me to, "Rub a little dirt in it!"
Mother's hands were rougher. She could turn a wrench, rig it up in a pinch. Cut a lawn on the weekend, early morning heat, Saturday cartoons, I'm never asleep. Come in red-faced sweating, hair in a band, throw open the door that cool air slaps skin cold. You chug an already opened can.
Late night, I come up slow and silent. The windows dark 'cept for the yellow glow, your lamp always low. Head bowed at your altar, these papers stack ever taller. His hands are softer, heart too, always aching with mind's anxieties. I creep past, to be alone.
When he calls out, I hurt with irritated timbre. These sounds cut and I feel it too, but can't seem to stoop to you, take alcohol and clean the wound, carefully place a
Bandage ever fixed on you.

I must be alone.
My cuts, not visible, are many. I've rubbed so
much dirt in, the worms have embedded
In skin.
Do I have the feminine?

68. Sunblind

I felt cold today. I haven't felt in weeks.
I wrote a line I'd written before,
Saw a tree like I hadn't ever,
Heard a song before I woke,
Thought of my end, and everyone's.
In lit pixels, I read of someone's death.
So much light upon our faces,
Like walking east at sunrise,
Sunblind.

69. Sunskin, Moonheart, Hailmind

Skin

The sun is welcome, but does it fit?
My disposition?
Is unsettled.
A welcomed sun can still burn,
And blister
This skin I'm in.
Smoldering.

Heart

This hail batters my empty heart with frozen
tears that no longer cry, just to sigh and
stare, walk for the wear, and no longer care.

Mind

This moon pulls mind away with its motion.
I rise and fall with the tide but fear this violent
ride.

Yes! I mind!
And will mind.
Until a time is set when a hollow heart held
beneath seared skin can live in the soft
Light, that silent night, peaceful and cooled.

70. To Stop and Go

To Stop.

Do you ever stop and think of me?
I do of you, though I wish it weren't true.
The deep dark tree bathed mountain, sky grey
blue, the chapel of my practice sits
across a great field of grass. The colossal trees,
ancient canopies, shade the dead.
Yellow brown green the moss creeps up their
crumbling stones, the well-worn paths muddy
from the endless wet, but don't fret. I feel great
calm as I stand here high
Above, observing this thought. Just a small
moment. To stop.

And Go?

The desire to linger is set in me. Whether here at
this godlike scene, nature and man in
The serene. What a beautiful gift, to take this
moment and lean against wood, stare no
Longer than I should, go? Breathe deep the
healing pleasure of this moment, and

remember it is only just a moment. Now go forward and push on. Whether or not others stop matters naught, when all it took was a thought.

71. Friend

Break my bones with your embrace!
I've missed you!
Endlessly pining, always rewinding, just to remind, I mind this solitude.
But now you're here! Sit with me!
I have so much to tell you!
If you can stand this epic, I'll spin it until the moon droops, your eyes drop, and my whole essence smiles wide, but softly, my eyes silently watching your peaceful rest.

72. A Soft Ache, This Hounding Agitation

A soft ache, this dull creep.
A slow descent into a weak dark sleep.
The dream spins and grasps at limbs only to turn
'round and fall again.
Down soft moan sighs never a satisfying bed.
The dread of this chord embodies my structures.
A head rest discordant the frame distorts it.
Creations of outside forces demand
consideration,
And anxiety grows with this undue
contemplation.
This hounding agitation.
A rhythmic dance chasing tails of transposed
clusters.
It's really all the same.
Lacking in any luster.
Life's ultimate bluster.
Now I feel flustered as heavy winds grow again.
They sing a hopeful melody amid the running
river rife with strife.

A swirling chaotic undertow, this deep doubled
voice drags until muscle gives in.
Fully destroyed, a final drop towards eruption.
Scream awake to self-destruction.

73. Song Bird

Yesterday I witnessed a most delightful sight. A beautiful blue bird landed on the line extending from my window, bowed its head and took a look at my life.

I froze in place as its subtle movements shut me down. I thought to grab my phone for a photo but quiet mind said, "No, look, with eyes that take infinite frames in timeless intervals." And so I disappeared lest the bird lift off in fright. I slipped away and watched my little blue friend hop to the window box and look in again. Those beady black eyes hide its soul. "Who are you blue bird? What's sent you my way? A gift for me today."

Then she hurried away. Of course, I couldn't know if she or he but I'd like to think that blue bird, you were a piece of her spirit sent for a simple hello. And who is she but a nameless, faceless, hopeless wish for something seeming not to exist. But your lovely dance about my dwelling has brought about this grandeur of delusion. I swell to fantastic conclusions.

Later I find you again sitting on the fence between the alley and my house. I watch your

stately stance upon t that barrier. I let my look
linger as I know if I turn back to life I'll just
find I've lost you to flight. And lo and behold as
the call pulled me away, I come to find my old
friend has flown and indeed I desire to throw
this window wide and jump into sky take my
own wing and sing straight up to heaven that
that blue bird has given me hope and a sign that
now's the time, Charlie Parker was right.
Blues in and blues out never you'll know if
you're sitting on the fence, staring out windows
at other's lives hoping for signs of what to do
from them, who, and who would know but yeah
I'm
Rolling now 'cause damn I know what it means
to be the bird and all the sounds I've heard the
Songs she sings they're coming out now in a
shatter crack ring the whole earth vibes with my
wind beat when I fly up to meet
My blue bird, true friend, lover of song. I must
see you again.

74. Tall Tales

Where are you now, sun?
My disposition is settled in
Hot humid wind I'm Texas again.
Raining heavy for once and then just like that
you turned to drizzly drop just to stop.
Oregon bipolar, now you're ramping up some
more but where's your storm?
I've already explicated my form.
I fill in for thunder when I scream the songs of
my younger years ago I now know the
Feeling of flashing, crackling, back breaking, the
sky splits as I rip a fire gold hot white
forked tongued spit. And all mixed up in the
brightest black night my shining lighthouse
pollutes nature's beauty as I shout my insides
from atop rock cliffs, passing ships drop
their sails and a hubris feeling slips into old
wood cracks form the salt spray sweat of ocean
wave slaps. I'm finally back. Bigger than all
God's and any Satan's darkest sin. I
stand up taller than the trees that opened my
eyes to the heavens within. And look out over
randomness beautification was it creation? But

now I take it and throw it back as my word and
sound all these things that I've found high above
and deepest low blow to the plexus sends a burn
wish for air, and an eye gape stare. But no.
From here I land the punches with solar wind
tails trailing their trajectory. And earthquake
rubble left from the deafening shake of which to
construct a better fate. I'll build a staircase to my
level if you have the legs to climb it's a damn
long way to reach mine. I need more heat.
Your wet cold is dragging these feet in drab
stagnant pools I feel like such an old fool
Up here all alone. Thinking I'm good. But the
rhymes are getting stale and I sense impending
Failure. If each time I grow taller how hard the
crash to follow.

75. Tired

I'm too tired to work,
Too awake to sleep,
Too mixed up to think.
If only I would drink.
A toke or two.
I want to run this one through.
To the End.
The day never done.
When is it won?

76. Justify Me Ye Space

When I was a young white boy the Pawnee
scared me.
But I wished to be a warrior like them.
Strength and will.
I wanted to dance with the wolves.
Not to be them or take of,
But to experience the freedom of danger.
What wolves has the white man danced with but
himself?
Or has he turned to mirror and seen his disgust.
Trust in self that your side is not side
but circle. Come round to find the end is never
and was not to be or a beginning never to see if
we could forget our greed. Our desire for endless
growth. What have we found but grasping and
rejecting? Let it go. Home is where you find
your spirit. That's the answer, white friend.
You're searching for our lost souls in cultures
who never lost theirs. Stop taking from others.
Go inside to find you divinity. Then can you
share with others and them with thee as breaking
bread is never left aloof when enemies sit and

listen. Go. Now make friends and see the change
as you become The. Not he or she, not me or I,
just-you, when we become just-us. Justice.
Serve it for those who deserve it.

77. Peace

I come in peace.
A mess of pieces.
But I now see.
What others told me
I believe
Because I knew
But now with clear view
I can move
Directed
I've over inspected
Self- centered hectic
But soon collected
I'll let go of the invective
I've come to expect it
So next time I'll vex it
Not me or you
Because I've seen through
I'm ready for what I have to do
Orange flowers bloom
October, harvest me soon.

78. This Holy Fire

I am not afraid
I have been made.
In this crucible
This Holy Fire
I could fill universes with these tears
Endless oceans of whale cries
Our everlong sigh.
This body alight
Ever in fire
Though drowned in desire
Ferry us this God I've finally seen
Make me the river man
I now understand
The smoke grows
The smolder keeps me
Alive
Though I feel older
I'm younger each day
Blow me away
The oxygen caress
Yes yes yes!
Stoke my fire
Stole in celestial spires.

79.   You're Elemental Necessity, Our Garden's Need

I love the feel of soot from the foot of a French
press best roast my God let us toast to this
bliss a kiss from
Your bean bitter the twist
Of tongue on that last rung
Sung through gritty teeth
The taste is actually sweet
When you listen within
The planted feed of our ever green need
Your pitter patter rain drop splatter of cloudy
mind
Your gusty hot blast of baneful intent
I'll listen
Blind me with your sun's ringing rays
I'll listen!
Because you're elemental!
Yes!
Absolutely essential!
And when you let it all go
That's when you'll know
It's how we grow.

In this garden of Eden
We're all little seedlings
Or maybe you're flowering
No matter the time
It's allowing
That freedom
To storm and scream, cry and dream, challenge
The scene, just be what it means to be
When you see that it's just you and me, me-you
That's Mu, all of us too. And that, friend,
Is the Godsend that cultivates and co-creates our
springing bloom.
It's always been right within.
When you look out,
Forget sin.
Just stop.
Listen.

80. Of Two Minds and Many, End with Enmity For Any Remedy

I'm of two minds. The romantic and the modern, but what of our current?
A feeling of fine struggle for breath just to discover, free of absurdity, the voice of sweetness and sin, dissonance and consonance all wrapped up in gold and glittered to gild our greedy self-centered trip up and down our turn 'round the run of time's rhyme.
Why do I find repeating the songs of yesteryears? We sought an end but seem to be only here again. In a pastiche of past politics and sound quips. All the short bits have rotted out the brain with ticks. But what of mine? The notes would harrow, and hope
For healing in bone marrow bread baked to a taste delight and least of all to dare them.
Feel inside the square and sacred only to believe, now naked, that God means what I've Shown from within when I stopped to listen

As dew entries jotting then dropping drip
Off the last lash hanging this flicking so fast
flaying eye sight , batter my single-son
individual-solitary-one no longer I fight the
sense of union in forgotten-self I ascend the
transmutation of my aberration, in shared
vision I see our reflection in its curve and
that's when   I heard, God in every silent
vibration, never a believer, but now I love the
sensation.

81. Thank You

Thank you for this breath I breathe,
These feet that still carry me.
This heart beats along stepping stones to forever
ago. I still feel the hurt I sowed. Why
must it grow? The cyclic season of my reasoning
mind running wide God I feel everything at once
and nothing comes but this hate for the end of it.
I just want to know if it could be a way to see
but for me I'm just here standing still singing my
heart always ringing this body alive for the final
time. But not in a rush I walk steady now, the
end is not the goal. It's the journey all the sights
and sounds the trees high and the dirt low like a
bird I can soar above it all but I must drop to my
knees peck at the earth just to eat. Balanced
between sky and soil this soul hurts, but isn't
that the point of it? To feel?   Something.
Anything. It's all real.
Just-feel.

82. O Ignis Caritatis

Early morning lungs ache from late night smoke.
I woke with a head full of snot
It's just a short walk
Till it empties into thought.
It's the time I take every day.
My seventh hour.
Bitter becomes the taste
But I love the sting of soft sun kisses
Thick phlegm ripped again
Spit
Down to 11 a little peace of 7th heaven
Another smoke and a coke.
A new morning ritual ever less healthy than
the last.
"Like end of the month peanut butter, spread
thin"
"I know that"
Damn do I remember when I fried up grilled
cheeses, sold books and games just for a bit
Of bread and some tuna, a 40 or two, 211
damn that's a quick way to heaven.
I let it all go 'cept it crept back up a little piece
at a time each circle rising as I descend my

levels but I will not touch bottom. No. The
bottle is straight fucking rotten.
I've been to it to know the top.
I had to stop.
That was the first love I let fly.
And each other followed til all I saw were
The darting swallows and crying scrub jays,
O! viridissima virga! I've known the feel of
green moss clung to bark so brownly dark the
gritty rub of sandpaper soil, the soft
Give of forest floor crinkling leaves snapping
twigs I bowed to your creatures as they
suckled my skin this blood within, my vow
now I fulfill as you taste my sin. And will it be
all that I've seen in this deep sleep state of
transcendent vision, all the stories and
decisions, your thorn bush trials, I've walked
a thousand miles! When is it enough? I thank
you for these tools you've given. This body I
love it feels amazing, this mind is crazy
But I've found the maze end. It's you. Tu,
candidum lilium. O ignis caritatis!

83. Angels

So many gloriously talented musicians have died young. And not just those sound
painters but wordsmiths, colorists, and body contortionists. Those who stop to help and tell stories. Great orators moving crowds forward, toward progressive actions. But what of the others? Mothers and fathers, sons and daughters those that are neither, but all the vibrant vibrating universal shake of our atoms deep. It's all and everything yes all and everything that has and will pass. I stop and wonder what might be of that unfulfilled potential? The great unknown of their burning sun's early expansion, flinging
nebulas into an aura surrounding their solid self, the universe alive with their vibrancy, our sky forever adorned with icons of the one true faith, Humanity. If just one more moment? What if? Just one? They left us feeling alone and done, but not for wanting.
Emtpy-handed?   No I'm burning in their fire rain. O, these little pieces of heaven!

(This piece is dedicated to Dralen Mason, and all those artists who've gone ahead of us on that journey into the final unknown. But not to forget our shared existence that no matter your station in life we are all angels and artists of His divinity.

84. Desire

I have wallowed in the dumpster of desire.
Searching soul to trash this longing.
Rubbish to rush in thronging but aye there is the
rub. For in that seeking sighing I have found but
treasures allying fruitlessness and not success.
No dress could cover this mess. No toil could
lance the boil. No sign in the stars, no moon of
any size could foretell desire's demise. Only
you, Jesu, joy of man's desiring.

85. Resist

The river has swollen
The banks bent and broken
This flood has stuck in me
An end sense of being
Washed and free
Oh I can see the tree tops
Still breath
Still trunks branch roots
To grounding
Amidst waves crashing
The thrashing persists
But I resist

86. What Might Be

Do not let your fear prevent you from finding
out what might be.
I have lived my life that way and, oh!
How I made it here despite that?
I don't even know.
Some taste of normal?
What does that mean?
I try to find
Stable ground I fall again
Always in a state of spin
But the moment when
All desire forgotten
I begin to sing
God's glory
In every moving thing
A Gust of wind
Bird chirp dawn
Finally I feel free in song
All fear gone to death
The selfless sea
What might be

87. An Epiphany

Once again, an epiphany becomes my undoing.
But a foundation laid brings the freedom of
broadened perspective.
I feel no pleasure
This is not pain
It is everything and nothing at once
The beginning
To keep it is our desire
Nothing can be owned
Only held
But not even
Just gasping
Only air found
What to push against?
But I?
I will stand still in this state
I will open my only closed eye
Fight this lonely night
Even for one glimpse of the light

88. You

You burn so brightly
No one is safe from your sun-
Light split through window panes of my vessel
Touches skin with tingling immediacy
And I'm floating lakes of fire
But this is heaven
No hell
Caused I'm biding time and hoping
Saying things unspoken
And forgetting it all
Cause we flow
And I Glow.

III. Afterword

Bruce C. Autry

89. Love's Fool

I thought I had known love before,
But, oh, what a fool I was!
Until you came through my door
Oh, what a fool I was!
I thought I had known the score,
But, oh, what a fool I was!
I thought I had known love more
Or less in the here and now
Until you brought eternity
In the moment when this fool
Heard you say "yes" and your smile
Taught me what real love was
And even now through my tears
I know what this fool felt
In that moment when you
Became the love beyond the wishing star
To which I chart my sailing on love's sea
Until we find each other again
In the safe harbor where fools
Have a wisdom tasting sweet upon the tongue.

www.ingramcontent.com/pod-product-compliance
Lightning Source LLC
Chambersburg PA
CBHW061347160726
47995CB00001B/205